FAMILY TREE

FAMILY TREE

Filling the Family Tree

by Jim Ollhoff

Visit us at
www.abdopublishing.com

Published by ABDO Publishing Company, 8000 West 78th Street, Suite 310, Edina, MN 55439.
Copyright ©2011 by Abdo Consulting Group, Inc. International copyrights reserved in all countries. No part of this book may be reproduced in any form without written permission from the publisher. ABDO & Daughters™ is a trademark and logo of ABDO Publishing Company.

Printed in the United States of America, North Mankato, Minnesota
052010
092010

Editor: John Hamilton
Graphic Design: Sue Hamilton
Cover Design: John Hamilton
Cover Photo: iStockphoto
Interior Photos: Ancestry.com-pgs 22 & 28; iStockphoto-pgs 1, 3, 6, 16, 18, 20, 27 & 32; Leister Productions/Reunion-pg 22; Library of Congress-pgs 24, 25, 26 & 29; RavenFire Media-pgs 5, 7, 9, 10, 11, 13, 15, 17, 19, 21 & 23; Thinkstock-pgs 4, 8, 11, 12 & 14

Library of Congress Cataloging-in-Publication Data

Ollhoff, Jim, 1959-
  Filling the family tree / Jim Ollhoff.
    p. cm. -- (Your family tree)
  Includes index.
  ISBN 978-1-61613-464-8
  1. Genealogy--Juvenile literature. I. Title.
  CS15.5.O45 2011
  929'.1--dc22
                          2009050806

Contents

The Family Tree

How did you get to be the way you are? How did you get to be you? In many ways, your parents, grandparents, and great-grandparents made you who you are. They not only passed down genes, but sometimes they passed down attitudes and values from family to family. You owe your life to your parents, grandparents, and great-grandparents.

One of the ways to discover who went before us is through the study of genealogy. And when it comes to the study of family history, the family tree is the most basic tool.

Family Tree

Paternal Grandfather
Birth Date:
Birth Place:
Married:
Place of Marriage:
Death Date:
Place of Death:
Place of Burial:

Father
Birth Date:
Birth Place:
Married:
Place of Marriage:
Death Date:
Place of Death:
Place of Burial:

Paternal Grandmother
Birth Date:
Birth Place:
Married:
Place of Marriage:
Death Date:
Place of Death:
Place of Burial:

You
Birth Date:
Birth Place:

Maternal Grandfather
Birth Date:
Birth Place:
Married:
Place of Marriage:
Death Date:
Place of Death:
Place of Burial:

Mother
Birth Date:
Birth Place:
Married:
Place of Marriage:
Death Date:
Place of Death:
Place of Burial:

Maternal Grandmother
Birth Date:
Birth Place:
Married:
Place of Marriage:
Death Date:
Place of Death:
Place of Burial:

Illustration 1 - Template
(Photocopy and Fill In)

Illustration 1 (page 5) is a basic family tree chart. You could photocopy it and use it to write up your own family. Illustration 2 (page 7) is another kind of family tree chart. It's called a fan chart. It is another way to see all the people who came before you.

But what if you don't have all the information you need to fill out a family tree or fan chart? What if you don't know all the names, dates, and cities? You may have to interview your grandparents or other family members. This book will give you some hints about what questions to ask.

Below: To fill in all the information on a genealogy chart, you may need to interview several members of your family.

Family Tree Fan Chart

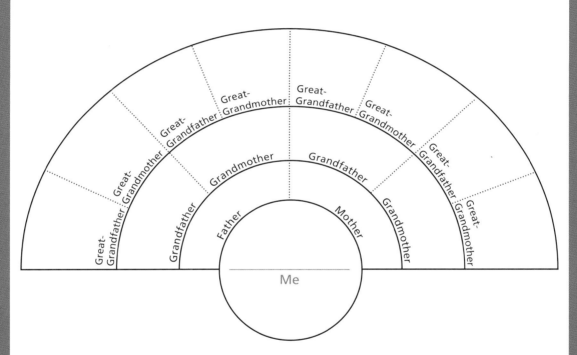

Father

Mother

Grandfather

Grandmother

Grandfather

Grandmother

Great-Grandfather

Great-Grandmother

Great-Grandfather

Great-Grandmother

Great-Grandfather

Great-Grandmother

Great-Grandfather

Great-Grandmother

Me

My Family

Illustration 2 - Template
(Photocopy and Fill In)

Interviewing Grandparents

You probably don't have enough information to completely fill out a family tree chart by yourself. That's where grandparents come in. Grandparents can be wonderful sources of information. So, the next step is to set up a time to interview them.

Illustration 3 (page 9) has a list of possible questions to ask your grandparents. If possible, talk to them in person or on the phone. Ask permission to record the conversation. Use the list of questions as conversation starters. Encourage them to share their recollections and their stories. When they share a story that helps you learn about the family, ask them to share more.

Inside their heads are wonderful, revealing stories about your family history. However, most people don't share those stories unless they are asked very specific questions. The record of those stories will be like gold someday, to you or your own children.

Questions for Your Grandparents

Grandparent's Name _____ Date Interviewed _____

When were you born? _____ Where were you born? _____

How many brothers and sisters did you have? _____

What are their names and birthdays? _____

What was your family like? _____

What are your earliest memories? _____

What did you or your family do for fun? _____

What was the happiest time in your life? _____

What kind of chores did you have to do as a child? _____

What kid of jobs did you have? _____

Did you serve in the military? Yes No When and where? _____

What was life like? _____

What kinds of things did you worry about? _____

What did you want to do when you grew up? _____

How did you meet Grandma/Grandpa? _____

What events really changed the course of your life? Why? _____

Their Parents

What were the names of your parents? _____

What was the maiden name of your mother? _____

When were they born? _____ Where were they born? _____

Do you know how they met? _____

When did they get married? _____

Where did they live? _____

What was their job? _____ Education? _____

What were they like? _____

When did they die? _____ Where are they buried? _____

Did they have any traditions or ways of doing things that you still do today? _____

What are some of your favorite stories about them? _____

Their Grandparents

What were the names of your grandparents? _____

What was the maiden name of your grandmother? _____

When were they born? _____ Where were they born? _____

When and where did they get married? _____

Do you remember what they looked like? _____

What were they like? _____

When did they die? _____ Where are they buried? _____

What are some of your recollections about them? _____

First Immigrants

Who was the first person in the family to come to this country? _____

Where did they come from? _____

Why did they come to this country? _____

Illustration 3 - Template (Photocopy and Fill In)

When you are finished with the conversation, put everything in order right away. If they have given you photographs, write down who is in the photograph. If they have given you a memento or souvenir, write down whom it came from and why it was important. Do it right away while the memory is still fresh. If you didn't record the conversation, then assemble your notes and write out as much of it as you can, before your

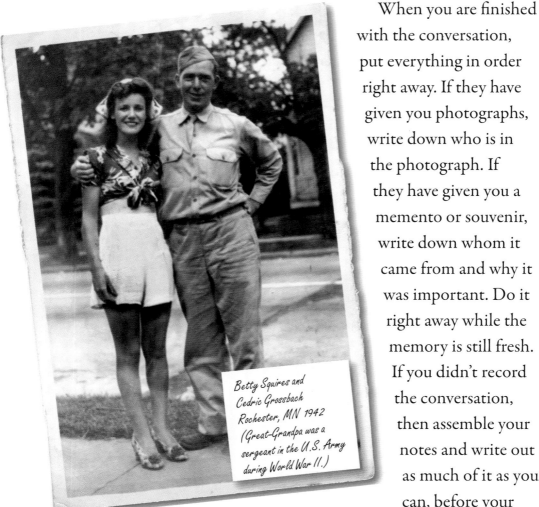

Betty Squires and Cedric Grossbach Rochester, MN 1942 (Great-Grandpa was a sergeant in the U.S. Army during World War II.)

Above: Be sure to write down who is in family photographs.

memory fades. If you recorded the conversation, then transcribe the interview. The conversation will be valuable someday to other members of the family.

Put the mementos in a special place where they won't get damaged. If they gave you a document or newspaper clipping, put it in an acid-free folder or acid-free plastic so that it won't degrade over time. If they gave you photos, you might want to scan them, since photograph colors begin to fade after a few decades.

Above: Put special photos, documents and mementos in acid-free plastic folders or albums.

Interviewing Others

Another step to take to help fill out your family tree is to interview uncles, aunts, and cousins. Interviewing others can often fill in the information for your family tree, particularly if your grandparents are no longer living. You might send some emails around or make some phone calls and see what kind of information emerges. Families often have someone who has already done some research on the family history, so you might get lucky and hit the jackpot.

Aunts and uncles often have great memories of your grandparents, and even great-grandparents. It's good to collect stories and recollections from others to help fill in the information. The stories help to make the people on the family tree more than just names and dates.

Illustration 4 (page 13) has some possible questions for other people that might help you fill in your family tree.

Below: Aunts, uncles, and cousins often have memories of your family members. It's a good idea to interview them.

Questions for Your Aunts, Uncles, and Cousins

Extended Family Member's Name _____

Relationship to You _____ Date Interviewed _____

When were you born? _____ Where were you born? _____
How many brothers and sisters do you have? _____
What are their names and birthdays? _____
How many children do you have? _____
What are their names and birthdays? _____
What was your family like? _____
What did you or your family do for fun? _____
What kind of chores did you have to do as a child? _____
What kind of jobs did you have? _____
What was life like? _____
What kinds of things did you worry about? _____
What did you want to do when you grew up? _____
What events really changed the course of your life? Why? _____
_____

Their Families
What were the names of your parents? _____
What was the maiden name of your mother? _____
When were they born? _____ Where were they born? _____
Do you know how they met? _____
When did they get married? _____
Where did they live? _____
What was their job? _____ Education? _____
What were they like? _____
When did they die? _____ Where are they buried? _____
Did they have any traditions or ways of doing things that you still do today? _____
What are some of your favorite stories about them? _____

Their Grandparents
Who were your grandparents? _____
What was the maiden name of your grandmother? _____
When were they born? _____ Where were they born? _____
When and where did they get married? _____
Do you remember what they looked like? _____
What were they like? _____
Are they still alive? _____ If no, where are they buried? _____
What are some of your recollections about them? _____

Illustration 4 - Template (Photocopy and Fill In)

13

Brothers, Stepsisters, and Second Cousins

Below: We are all related to many people.

We are all related to many people. We call them siblings, stepsiblings, cousins, second cousins, and many other titles.

Illustration 5 (page 15, top) shows the relationships between people when one parent has had more than one spouse. This is sometimes called a blended family, or stepfamily.

Illustration 6 (page 15, bottom) shows uncles and aunts. Brothers of our parents are our uncles. Sisters of our parents are our aunts.

Relationships: What's a stepsibling?

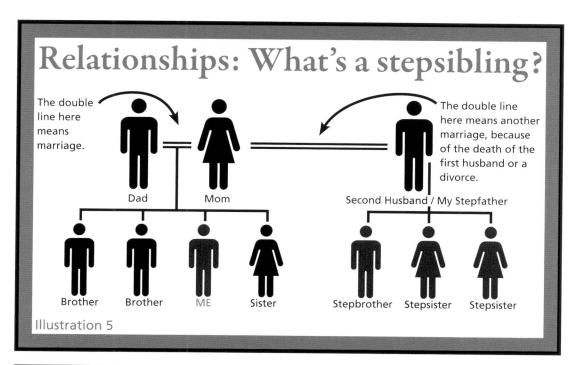

The double line here means marriage.

The double line here means another marriage, because of the death of the first husband or a divorce.

Dad — Mom — Second Husband / My Stepfather

Brother — Brother — ME — Sister — Stepbrother — Stepsister — Stepsister

Illustration 5

Relationships: What's an Uncle & Aunt?

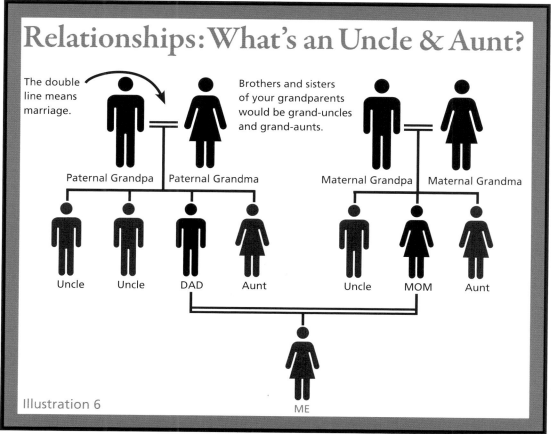

The double line means marriage.

Brothers and sisters of your grandparents would be grand-uncles and grand-aunts.

Paternal Grandpa — Paternal Grandma — Maternal Grandpa — Maternal Grandma

Uncle — Uncle — DAD — Aunt — Uncle — MOM — Aunt

ME

Illustration 6

Illustration 7 (page 17) shows cousins. The children of our uncles and aunts are our first cousins. The children of our cousins are our "first cousins once removed." The "once removed" title means that there is a generation removed from us. The grandchildren of our first cousins are our "first cousins twice removed." For every generation that is further away from you, it is another generation removed.

Relationships: What's a Cousin Once Removed?

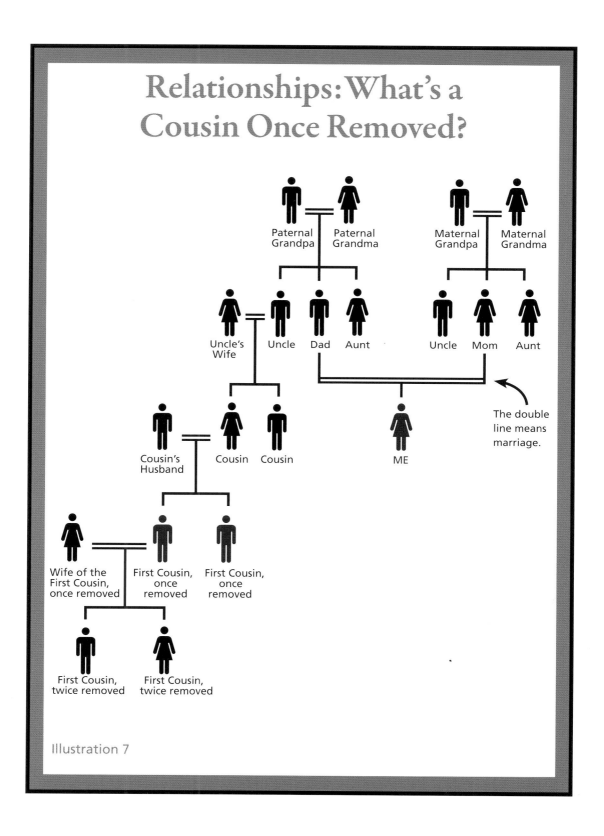

Illustration 7

Illustration 8 (page 19) shows the definition of a first cousin, second cousin, and third cousin. When a person has children, and that person's first cousin has children, the children are second cousins. For each generation that goes down from the common ancestor, the children are "further away" from first cousins.

The parents of our grandparents are called great-grandparents. The grandparents of our grandparents are called great-great-grandparents. For each generation that goes further back in history, we add a "great." Sometimes this is abbreviated with a number and the letter "G." Your great-great-great-great-grandfather is your 4G-grandfather.

Right: Your great-great-grandmother would be abbreviated 2G-grandmother.

Relationships:
What's a Cousin?

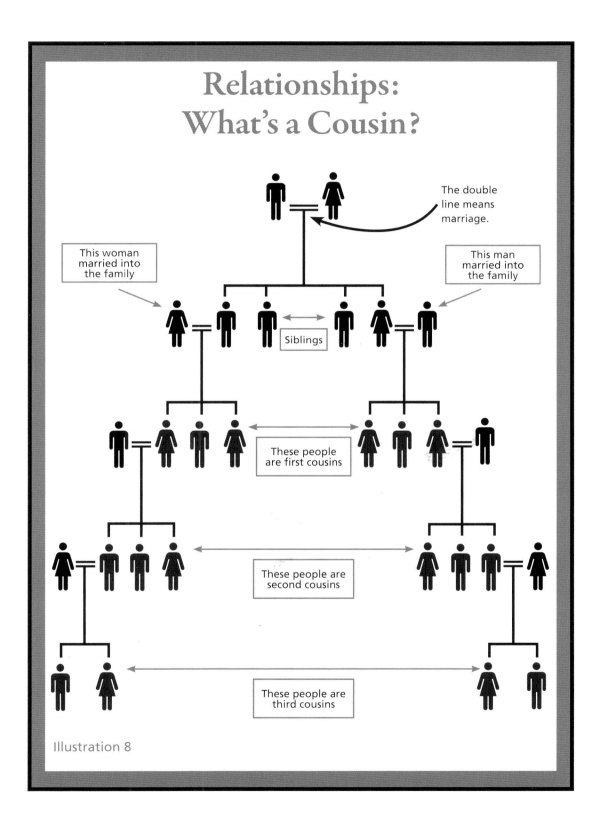

The double line means marriage.

This woman married into the family

This man married into the family

Siblings

These people are first cousins

These people are second cousins

These people are third cousins

Illustration 8

Drawing an Extended Family Tree

An extended family tree, also called a collateral family tree, is created when we add children of brothers, sisters, and cousins. A direct ancestor family tree starts with an individual and builds up through their parents, their parents' parents, and so on. An extended family tree instead starts with one couple, and builds through their children, their children's children, and so on. It can get very large and complicated very quickly. When you show all the people descended from grandpa and grandma, the number of people can quickly grow into the hundreds. Extended family trees are remarkable tools to show people the impact of one couple.

There are no right or wrong ways to do an extended family tree, but Illustration 9 (page 21) shows one way. Extended family trees are often done with the oldest generation at the top, rather than on the right side of the page. It is customary to list all the children, even ones who died in infancy or at birth.

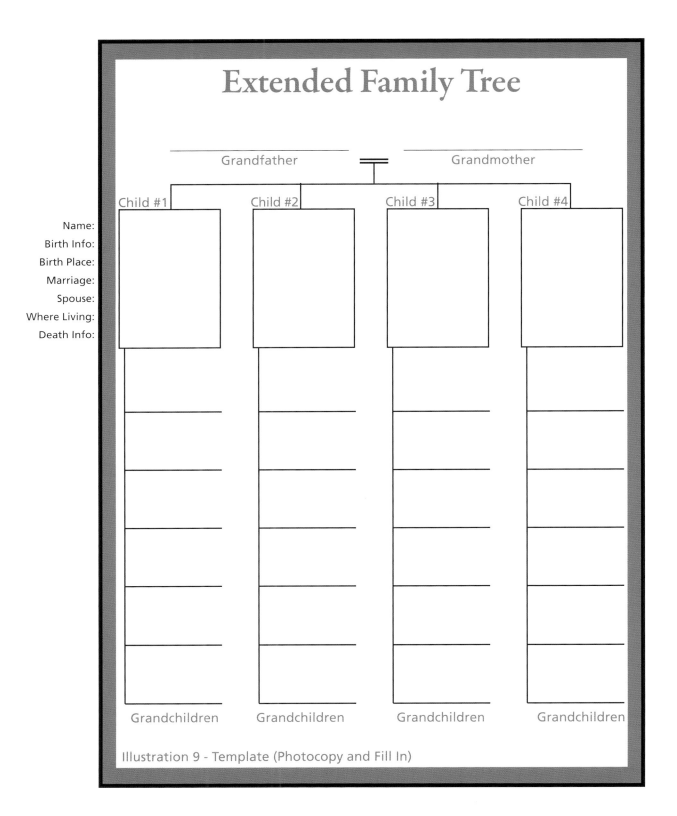

Extended Family Tree

Grandfather ══ Grandmother

Child #1   Child #2   Child #3   Child #4

Name:
Birth Info:
Birth Place:
Marriage:
Spouse:
Where Living:
Death Info:

Grandchildren   Grandchildren   Grandchildren   Grandchildren

Illustration 9 - Template (Photocopy and Fill In)

21

It might be helpful to have just the names on an extended family tree, and then list important information elsewhere. The other information regarding birth, marriage, and death could be listed on a separate sheet, such as in Illustration 10 (page 23).

If you have genealogy software, it will organize the information for you. You might have less flexibility with how it's organized, but it should keep all the information you need in one handy place.

Right: Genealogy software can help organize your information for you. There are several different programs available.

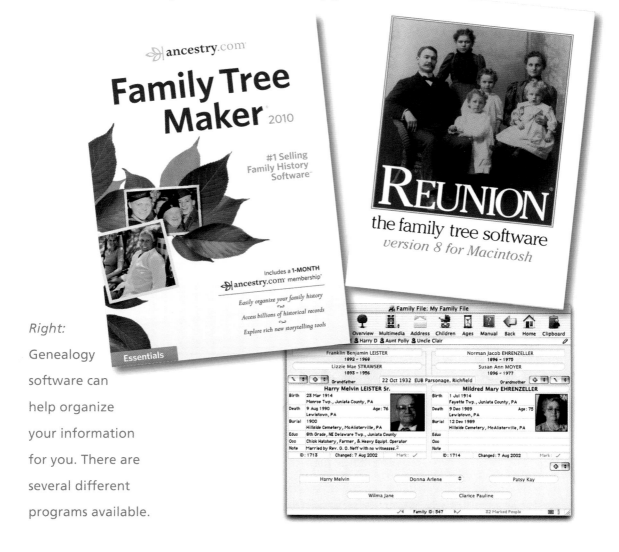

Family Information Sheet

Father:
Birth Date:
Birth Place:
Marriage Date:
Marriage Place:
Death Date:
Internment:

Mother:
Birth Date:
Birth Place:
Marriage Date:
Marriage Place:
Death Date:
Internment:

Child #1:
Birth Date and Place:
Marriage Date and Place:
Name of Spouse:
Occupation
Names of Children:
Death Date and Internment:

Child #2:
Birth Date and Place:
Marriage Date and Place:
Name of Spouse:
Occupation
Names of Children:
Death Date and Internment:

Child #3:
Birth Date and Place:
Marriage Date and Place:
Name of Spouse:
Occupation
Names of Children:
Death Date and Internment:

Child #4:
Birth Date and Place:
Marriage Date and Place:
Name of Spouse:
Occupation
Names of Children:
Death Date and Internment:

Illustration 10 - Template (Photocopy and Fill In)

Helpful Hints for the Family Tree

Below: Write a woman's name using her maiden name. A nickname can be added in parentheses.

Here are some hints that will help you as you are gathering information about your family members.

Write It Down

When you interview people, write down what they say, and who said it. If Grandpa Farnsworth told you that 4G-Grandma Julia was the first of the family to come to this country, then write down that Grandpa Farnsworth said so. Later, you can check his story with immigration records. Always cite your sources so that you know where the information came from.

Use Full Names

When writing the family tree, use a person's given name, and for women use their maiden name (the name before they were married). If someone has a nickname, put that nickname in parentheses next to the given name.

Yelana Anya Sokolov ("Lena") 1870

24

Grandpa Farnsworth said that 4G-Grandma Julia was the first member of the family to come to America from Germany. According to Immigration Records, she arrived in the Port of New York on June 14, 1856, on the ship Luiska. She was 20 years old.

COPYRIGHT 1894, C. R. DODGE.

Above: When you interview people, write down what they say and who said it.

Above: Family lore is often incorrect. For example, one family's story was passed down that their 4G-grandfather met Abraham Lincoln. However, upon examining the grandfather's birth certificate, it was discovered that he was born in 1869. Lincoln was killed in 1865, four years before the grandfather was even born.

Don't Accept Lore As Fact

Family lore, or the oral stories of a family, can be a wonderful source of information. Family lore can tell us about our ancestors, who they were, and how they lived. However, family lore is often incorrect when it comes to facts. Don't treat lore as fact unless you have a primary, official document, like a birth certificate, to back up the story. You should identify that the story came from family lore until you find documentation.

Don't Make Assumptions

Just because you find someone with the same surname, or last name, as you, don't assume you are related to that person. Even if you have an uncommon surname, and the person comes from the same city as you, don't make an assumption unless you can prove it. Treat it as "a possible connection," not a fact.

Beware Of Scams

There are plenty of organizations out there that will sell you "your family tree," which is just a list of your surname, drawn from phone books. There are people who will write books about "your genealogy," which are simply Internet searches of your family name. Creating a family tree takes time, energy, and good detective skills. Don't be fooled by scams.

Consider Computer Software

When creating a family tree, especially an extended family tree, computer software can help you organize the huge numbers of names and dates that you will collect. There is also a way to share genealogical information on the Internet, called GEDCOM. It stands for GEnealogical Data COMmunication. It gives basic information, such as birth, marriage, death, and so on. The tags and data in the files can be read by most other genealogical software.

Do Your Research

Research your information thoroughly, and do it carefully. There's nothing worse for a genealogist than to find and use incorrect information. Check and double-check your facts. Prove everything and cite your sources. If you can't prove it, clearly identify that this information is tentative, from family lore, or only a possible link.

Above: Check and double-check your family facts.

What's Next?

Below: A page from the Connecticut Town Death Records, pre-1870. This is the type of primary document you can use to discover your forgotten ancestors.

You've interviewed your grandparents and some of your relatives. You've started building a family tree, maybe even an extended family tree. You've collected wonderful stories of the people who've come before you. But creating the family tree is only the first step in your genealogical research.

Next, you will go back further in history. Start looking for primary documents—the documents written at that time. Primary documents include birth records, marriage certificates, journals, and letters. There are hundreds of places to look for your ancestors!

You'll be starting to look for your forgotten ancestors, those who were gone long before the previous generation. You may find that there is no family lore before a certain point. It's like there is a wall keeping you from seeing the past. The next step in genealogy is to break through that wall using primary documents.

Looking further back in time is a way to remember your family's history. Your family started long ago. You goal is to help your family continue to honor those who came before you.

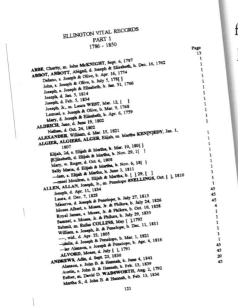

Above: In 1937, the Official Custodian of Census Records discovered people's ages whose births had not been registered. By reviewing primary records, such as old censuses, church records, and family Bibles, you may find missing information on your ancestors.

Glossary

ANCESTORS

The people from whom you are directly descended. Usually this refers to people in generations prior to your grandparents.

BLENDED FAMILY

A family that is formed when a current husband and wife have had children with another partner. All biological members of the family are combined to create a blended family. Also called a stepfamily.

COLLATERAL FAMILY TREE

See Extended Family Tree.

EXTENDED FAMILY TREE

A family tree that shows brothers, sisters, cousins, and their children. Also called a collateral family tree.

FAMILY TREE

A way of showing you, your parents, grandparents, and previous generations.

FAN CHART

A way of drawing up a family tree.

GEDCOM

A method of computer formatting designed to share genealogical information over the Internet.

GENEALOGY

The study of your ancestors and your family history.

INTERNMENT

The final resting place of a dead person's body or ashes, such as a cemetery, tomb, or urn.

LORE

The spoken stories that have been passed down from previous generations.

MATERNAL

Having to do with the mother's side of the family. Your maternal grandmother is your mother's mother.

MEMENTO

An object that may remind someone of a special person or event.

PATERNAL

Having to do with the father's side of the family. Your paternal grandmother is your father's mother.

SOUVENIR

An object that is kept as a reminder of a special person, place, or event.

SPOUSE

The person another person is married to. A husband or wife.

SURNAME

A person's last name.

Index

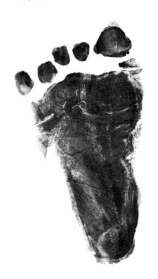
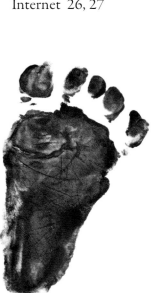